Selfish Sophie

by Damian Kelleher

Illustrated by Georgie Birkett

W
FRANKLIN WATTS
LONDON•SYDNEY

This edition 2009

Franklin Watts
338 Euston Road
London
NW1 3BH

Franklin Watts Australia
Level 17/207 Kent Street
Sydney
NSW 2000

A CIP catalogue record for this book is available
from the British Library.

ISBN 978 0 7496 9144 8

Series Editor: Louise John
Series Advisor: Dr Barrie Wade
Series Designer: Jason Anscomb

Printed in China

Franklin Watts is a division of
Hachette Children's Books,
an Hachette UK company.
www.hachette.co.uk

For Sophie - D.K

Sophie wasn't very good at sharing.

She didn't like to share
her sweets.

Or her books.

Or her cuddly toys.

Or any of her things!

"You know, it's much more fun to share your things," said Sophie's dad.

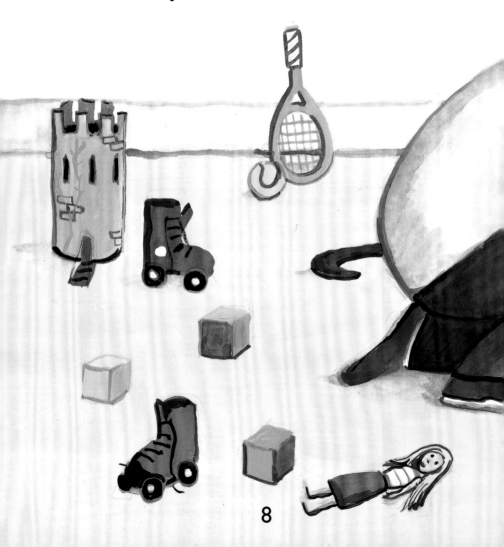

"They're mine!" said Sophie.

"And no one else can play with them."

Sophie's class went on a
trip to the zoo.

Sophie sat all by herself
on the coach.

"No one is sharing my seat," said Sophie.

Everyone else sat in pairs and sang songs.

"No one is sharing my lunch," said Sophie.

Everyone else shared their crisps and sandwiches.

After a while, it started to
rain. It poured and poured.

Everyone got out their umbrellas.

Everyone except Sophie.

Jake was by himself, too.

"Would you like to share my umbrella?" asked Jake.

"Yes, please," said Sophie.

"I'm getting very wet."

On the coach, Sophie and Jake shared a seat.

27

And they giggled all the
way home!

Puzzle 1

Put these pictures in the correct order.
Now tell the story in your own words.
How short can you make the story?

Puzzle 2

greedy   mean

excited

patient   worried

happy

kind   caring

selfish

Choose the words which best describe each character. Can you think of any more? Pretend to be one of the characters!

Answers

Puzzle 1

The correct order is:

1e, 2c, 3b, 4f, 5d, 6a

Puzzle 2

Sophie: greedy, mean

Dad: patient, worried

Jake: caring, kind

Look out for more Leapfrog stories:

The Little Star
ISBN 978 0 7496 3833 7

Recycled!
ISBN 978 0 7496 4388 1

Jack's Party
ISBN 978 0 7496 4389 8

The Crying Princess
ISBN 978 0 7496 4632 5

Jasper and Jess
ISBN 978 0 7496 4081 1

The Lazy Scarecrow
ISBN 978 0 7496 4082 8

Big Bad Blob
ISBN 978 0 7496 7092 4*
ISBN 978 0 7496 7796 1

Cara's Breakfast
ISBN 978 0 7496 7093 1*
ISBN 978 0 7496 7797 8

Croc's Tooth
ISBN 978 0 7496 7799 2

The Magic Word
ISBN 978 0 7496 7096 2*
ISBN 978 0 7496 7800 5

Tim's Tent
ISBN 978 0 7496 7801 2

Why Not?
ISBN 978 0 7496 7094 8*
ISBN 978 0 7496 7798 5

Sticky Vickie
ISBN 978 0 7496 7986 6

Handyman Doug
ISBN 978 0 7496 7987 3

Billy and the Wizard
ISBN 978 0 7496 7985 9

Sam's Spots
ISBN 978 0 7496 7976 7*
ISBN 978 0 7496 7984 2

Bill's Baggy Trousers
ISBN 978 0 7496 3829 0

Bill's Bouncy Shoes
ISBN 978 0 7496 7990 3

Little Joe's Big Race
ISBN 978 0 7496 3832 0

Little Joe's Balloon Race
ISBN 978 0 7496 7989 7

Felix on the Move
ISBN 978 0 7496 4387 4

Felix and the Kitten
ISBN 978 0 7496 7988 0

The Cheeky Monkey
ISBN 978 0 7496 3830 6

Cheeky Monkey on Holiday
ISBN 978 0 7496 7991 0

For details of all our titles go to: www.franklinwatts.co.uk